Based on the novel by Victor Hugo

Adapted by
Mary Sebag-Montefiore

Illustrated by Alfredo Belli

Edited by Lesley Sims
Designed by Samantha Barrett
Reading consultant: Alison Kelly

Contents

The characters in the story

Bishop Bienvenu
a bishop who gives his money to the poor

Valjean
a convict, prison numbers 24601 and 9430

Inspector Javert
a police officer and ex-prison guard

Père Madeleine
a mysterious factory owner who becomes Mayor of the town of Montreuil

Fantine

a factory worker

Cosette

Fantine's daughter, taken in by the Thénardiers

Monsieur Thénardier

an inn-keeper

Madam Thénardier

the inn-keeper's wife

Marius

a student and revolutionary

Eponine

the daughter of the Thénardiers

Prologue
Who is Valjean?

"THE WORLD IS ILL! People are dying from poverty. I swear to dedicate my life to curing this terrible disease." This was the vow of a French bishop in the nineteenth century.

His name was Bienvenu. He gave all his valuables to the poor, except for one pair of silver candlesticks and his silver knives and forks, which he couldn't bear to part with.

About to enter his life, coming nearer and nearer, was a vagabond, though at this stage neither knew of the other's existence.

The vagabond's name was Valjean.

Valjean's clothes were ragged, his feet bare, his face twisted in anger. How does a man get to be like this?

He was born to a very poor family. His parents died when he was young, leaving eight little children.

As he grew older, he tried to feed them. One hard winter, there was no work, and no food, so he smashed a window and stole a loaf. One small loaf. For that, he was caught and sent to prison.

He was locked up for years, no longer Jean Valjean but simply prisoner 24601. When he was released, he was like a full-blown storm raging with HATRED.

Chapter 1
The Choice

Valjean stumbled into a village and knocked at an inn door. "Can I have a room for the night? And food? I can pay."

"Certainly. Show me your identity papers," said the innkeeper.

Valjean handed over a yellow card.

The innkeeper saw it and glared. "I have no room free for jailbirds," he snapped.

"Then put me in the stable," Valjean begged.

"Impossible. The horses take up all the room."

"Please...I've been walking all day. I'm dropping with hunger. I need food."

"I've nothing to spare," said the innkeeper.

"Please...just a glass of water."

The innkeeper frowned. "A bullet's what you'll get if you don't leave now."

Valjean tried every inn in the district, but no one would help him.

Late that night, Bienvenu heard banging on his door. When he opened it, he saw a stranger who snarled, “I’ve knocked on hundreds of doors, but no one will help me. Don’t suppose you can either. I’m a convict on parole. I’ve been in prison for nineteen years. Five years for robbery with violence. Fourteen years for four attempts to escape. ‘A very dangerous man.’ That’s what it says on my yellow card. My name is Valjean.”

“My house is yours,” said Bienvenu. “Come in. Share my food. I know your name already.”

“How could you know my name?”

“Your name is ‘brother’,” said the bishop.

That night, Valjean, his stomach full, lay in a clean, warm bed. He wasn't used to being so comfortable and he couldn't sleep. He kept thinking of Bienvenu's silver knives and forks. They gleamed in his mind, just as they'd glittered on the table at supper.

He couldn't take any more. He slipped out of bed, dressed, crept downstairs, helped himself to the silver, and ran silently out into the darkness.

The next morning, Bienvenu answered another knock on his door. Three policemen stood on the doorstep, surrounding Valjean.

"Ah, my friend Valjean!" Bienvenu beamed. "I am glad you took the knives and forks. But you forgot the candlesticks. They are yours too."

"But he looked like a thief in his rags, with that sack full of silver!" spluttered the chief policeman.

"Well, he is not a thief," Bienvenu declared.

My possessions belong to the poor, Bienvenu was thinking. *And this man is one of them.*

Aloud, he said, "My brother, I have bought your soul and I give it to God."

All day, Valjean plunged through the countryside, as though he was still on the run. The bishop's forgiveness had almost...not quite, but almost...shaken his hatred.

That evening, he met a little boy walking towards him, tossing a coin and catching it again. And then he dropped it.

Valjean covered it with his foot.

"Monsieur, may I have my coin?" asked the boy.

"What's your name?"

"Petit-Jean."

"Get lost, Petit-Jean," said Valjean.

"But monsieur, my money!" cried Petit-Jean, beginning to sob.

Brandishing his stick, Valjean shoved it in the boy's face, yelling, "Go!"

The boy ran. Valjean could hear his sobs as he vanished from sight.

In the silent, dark evening, a strange new realization hit Valjean.

I have robbed a child.

"PETIT-JEAN!" he called.

No answer.

What had Bienvenu said? I give your soul to God.

With painful insight, Valjean suddenly understood Bienvenu. The bishop believed in the goodness of mankind. And, after that loving forgiveness, he – Valjean – had robbed a child.

He saw his own mind divided. On the one hand was hatred; on the other, a glimmering awareness that he could cast the hatred aside... forever. The choice:

...**EVIL**...?

...**GOOD**...?

was his alone.

He knelt, weeping... and felt his old self dissolve into nothingness.

Chapter 2
Cosette and Fantine

Years passed. Far away from the village where Valjean had met Bienvenu, lay the city of Montreuil. Here, a stranger had started a factory making jewels out of glass. This stranger, who was called Père Madeleine, had become a rich man. He paid high wages, spreading prosperity and happiness throughout the city. He was so admired that he was elected Mayor.

Everybody loved him, although he made Javert, the policeman, uneasy. *I wonder if he's hiding something,* Javert thought. *He seems too good to be true. Does he have a criminal past? I'm sure I recognize him from somewhere. I never forget a face. WHERE did I meet him? Maybe when I was a prison guard...*

One day, when Père Madeleine was walking through the town, he saw an old man, Fauchelevent, trapped under a cart.

"I can't breathe! I'm dying! Someone help me," gasped Fauchelevent.

Père Madeleine crouched by the cart and heaved it up to release him.

Javert had seen the whole thing. “I only know of one other man who had such strength,” he said, staring hard at Père Madeleine. “A convict named Valjean. Four times he escaped from prison.”

Père Madeleine said nothing.

Fauchelevent survived, but he wasn’t very strong, so Madeleine found him a gentle job as a gardener in a convent.

One of Madeleine's factory workers, Fantine, had a little girl, Cosette. Fantine couldn't work and look after her, so she paid the Thénardier family, who kept an inn in Montfermeil, to care for her. Fantine sent them all her wages for Cosette's keep.

"This child is a gold mine!" chuckled Monsieur and Madame Thénardier, and wrote urgent letters to Fantine. "Cosette is ill...she needs expensive medicines." "Cosette has grown; she needs a new coat!" "MORE money! MORE! MORE! MORE!"

The Thénardiers' daughter, Eponine, had lovely toys, clothes and food, while Cosette ate scraps, shivering in her rags. She had to scrub floors, sweep the yard and wash dishes. If she was slow, they beat her. Cosette's eyes, huge with unhappiness, overshadowed her frightened little face, but Fantine had no idea how her child was treated. All Fantine knew was that the Thénardiers constantly needed more money from her.

Fantine sold her hair, her clothes, then, agonizingly, her front teeth. With her wispy hair, old clothes, and her mouth dripping blood, she looked a fright. An officer saw her and laughed. Then he picked up some snow...

"AAAHHHH!" screamed Fantine, ripping his face with her fingernails. The officer punched her, and the noise brought Javert running.

"You'll get six months for brawling in the street, woman," he announced, hauling her into the police station.

"Please, have mercy..." pleaded Fantine, but Javert was immovable. She'd hurt an officer. She had to be punished. That was the law.

Javert hadn't noticed Père Madeleine following a little way behind them.

"This poor woman works in my factory," said Madeleine. "Release her. As Mayor, I have the power to make you."

"That's not justice," muttered Javert furiously, but he had to obey.

"I wish you'd asked me straight away for help. What brought you so low?" Madeleine asked Fantine, as he helped her from the police station.

"My little Cosette. I need money for her," Fantine explained.

Madeleine listened to her story. "This is all wrong. That family sounds suspicious to ask for so much money. I'll bring her back to you. Don't worry about anything. I'll pay whatever it takes."

He wrote a letter, and asked Fantine to sign it:

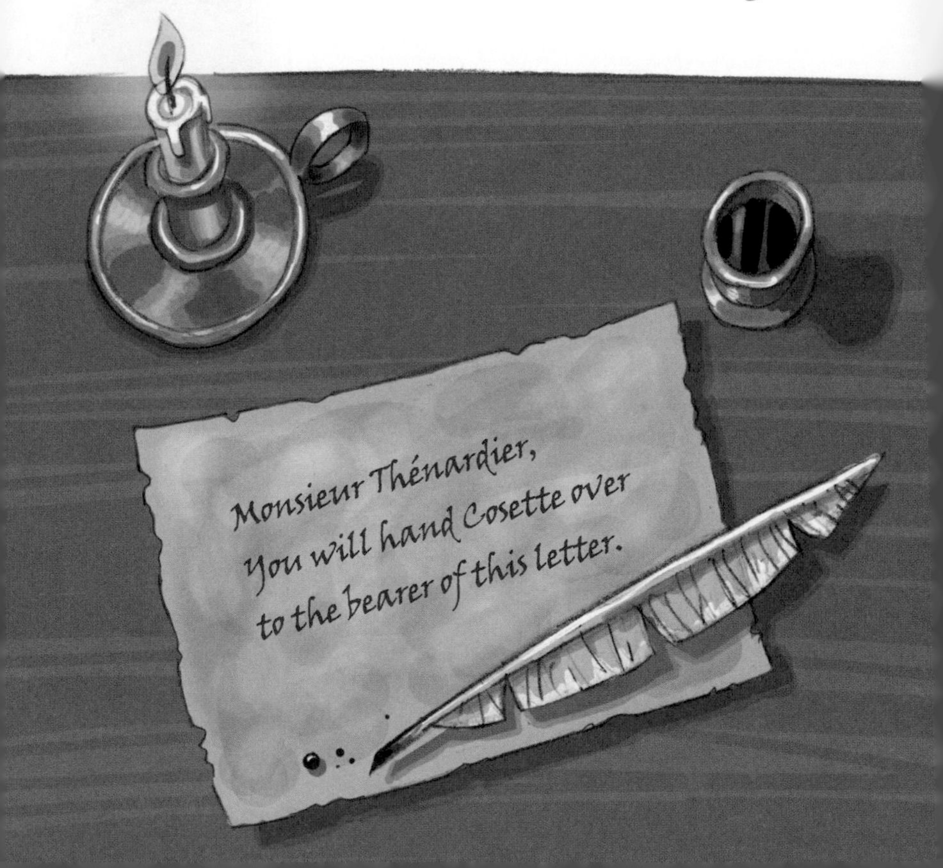
Monsieur Thénardier,
You will hand Cosette over
to the bearer of this letter.

Fantine signed...and fainted. Her ordeal had been too much for her. Madeleine took her to a hospital, where she lay in bed, warm and clean at last, yearning for Cosette.

"I'll see her tomorrow...my baby!" she murmured restlessly.

But that night, fever and weakness raged through her body, brought on by months of starvation, poverty and worry.

In the morning, the doctor shook his head. "She's dying... She has a day or two at most. I pray she lives long enough to see her child."

Just as Madeleine was setting off to collect Cosette, Javert marched into his house.

"I have committed a crime, Mayor. I should be punished," he declared. "Please recommend my dismissal from the police force."

"What have you done?"

"I denounced you."

Madeleine laughed. "To whom did you denounce me?"

"To the chief of police in Paris. I said you were an ex-convict. I told him your real name is Valjean. I knew Valjean years ago when I was a prison guard. You look like him. You have the same great strength. After he left prison he robbed a bishop and stole money from a small boy. The police have been looking for him ever since. But I was crazy to think he was you. The real Valjean has been found at last."

"Oh?" said Madeleine, his face blank, watching the candles burn in his silver candlesticks. The candlesticks the bishop had given him.

"Yes, he's been arrested for stealing apples. He keeps saying he's called Champmathieu, not Valjean. But two ex-convicts, his cell-mates from all those years ago, recognize him. He'll get life imprisonment this time. He's to be tried tomorrow, at Arras. I'm a witness. You must dismiss me for suspecting you."

"No. Javert. You are a decent man. Let this matter rest here."

Chapter 3
Back to Prison

Javert left, leaving Madeleine to his turbulent thoughts.

When Javert had begun speaking, Madeleine was tempted to shout, "I AM VALJEAN!"

Because...

...he'd dedicated his life to doing good. And an innocent man would be tried tomorrow.

Stay silent insisted another voice in his head.

Because...

...he'd repented; he'd been reborn...why disturb his new-found peace?

They've found their man, he thought. *That bloodhound, Javert, sniffing at my heels, won't trouble me any more. I'm safe!*

...It's fate...

If I confess, I'll go to prison. How can I do good if I'm locked up?

But...if I keep quiet, I'll rob an innocent man of his freedom.

Do I condemn him to save myself?

As he agonized, he seemed to see the old bishop's eyes upon him.

And he knew...

...knew that anything less than the absolute truth was abominable. The truth was a terrible prospect. Dreadful. Irretrievable. The ultimate sacrifice...

...but it had to be done.

Goodbye to freedom. Goodbye to being Mayor, to doing good, to respect. Farewell to listening to birdsong, to walking in the fields, giving pennies to children.

Gone, all that...

First, he hid his candlesticks, burying them in some woods together with a wallet stuffed with money and the letter Fantine had signed about Cosette. Then he jumped on his horse and cantered, as fast as he could, to Arras.

Valjean arrived at the courthouse spattered in mud and exhausted. He opened the door; he was inside the courtroom.

The prisoner in the dock had the same wary eyes, the same blaze of anger he once had.

O God, am I to become that again? he thought.

"I'm not Valjean. I'm Champmathieu," the prisoner was insisting.

Two witnesses, Brevet and Chenildieu, were sworn in.

"We were in prison with this man," they said. "He is Valjean."

As the judge pronounced: "The case appears proved," he was interrupted by a deafening cry from Madeleine.

"I AM VALJEAN!"

The courtroom fell silent.

Madeleine continued steadily. "I recognize you, Brevet. I remember your tattoo, a date, March 1st, 1815. Pull up your sleeve. Show it."

Trembling, the witness obeyed. The date was there for all to see.

"And you, Chenildieu. You have a scar on your right shoulder."

"It's true," whispered Chenildieu.

Valjean turned to the judge. "Do you believe me? I am Valjean."

What followed was inevitable. Javert sprang forward to clamp Madeleine in handcuffs, the judge gave him a life sentence and guards led him to the lock-up.

…And what of Fantine, weeping for Cosette?

She died.

Just before she died, she heard a workman's child running and laughing outside the hospital, a chance event that so often accompanies tragedy.

"My Cosette…" whispered Fantine.

Her head relaxed on her pillow and she breathed slowly…slowly…

She was buried in a pauper's grave, alongside other bones in the vast community of the poor.

Valjean returned to prison: Prisoner No. 9430. His hair had turned white with the shock of being back in jail. He looked like an old man.

Back in Montreuil, his factory was closed, followed by lower wages and unemployment. All the good he had done blew away, like ashes in the wind.

After nine months, he was sent as part of a prison work gang to serve on board the ship, *Orion*.

One day, a sailor was stuck on the rigging. He'd slipped; one foot caught on the ropes; below his dangling body, the sea churned. Horrified, the crew stared. The man would fall and drown.

No one dared risk his life to save him.

But wait! Someone was climbing the rigging. His cap flew off, showing white hair. Was this an old man, then?

Up he went, released the sailor who safely reached the deck, and then... he fell, vanishing into the waves. They tried to find his body, but it had disappeared, sunk into the ocean depths. Drowned.

It was prisoner 9430.

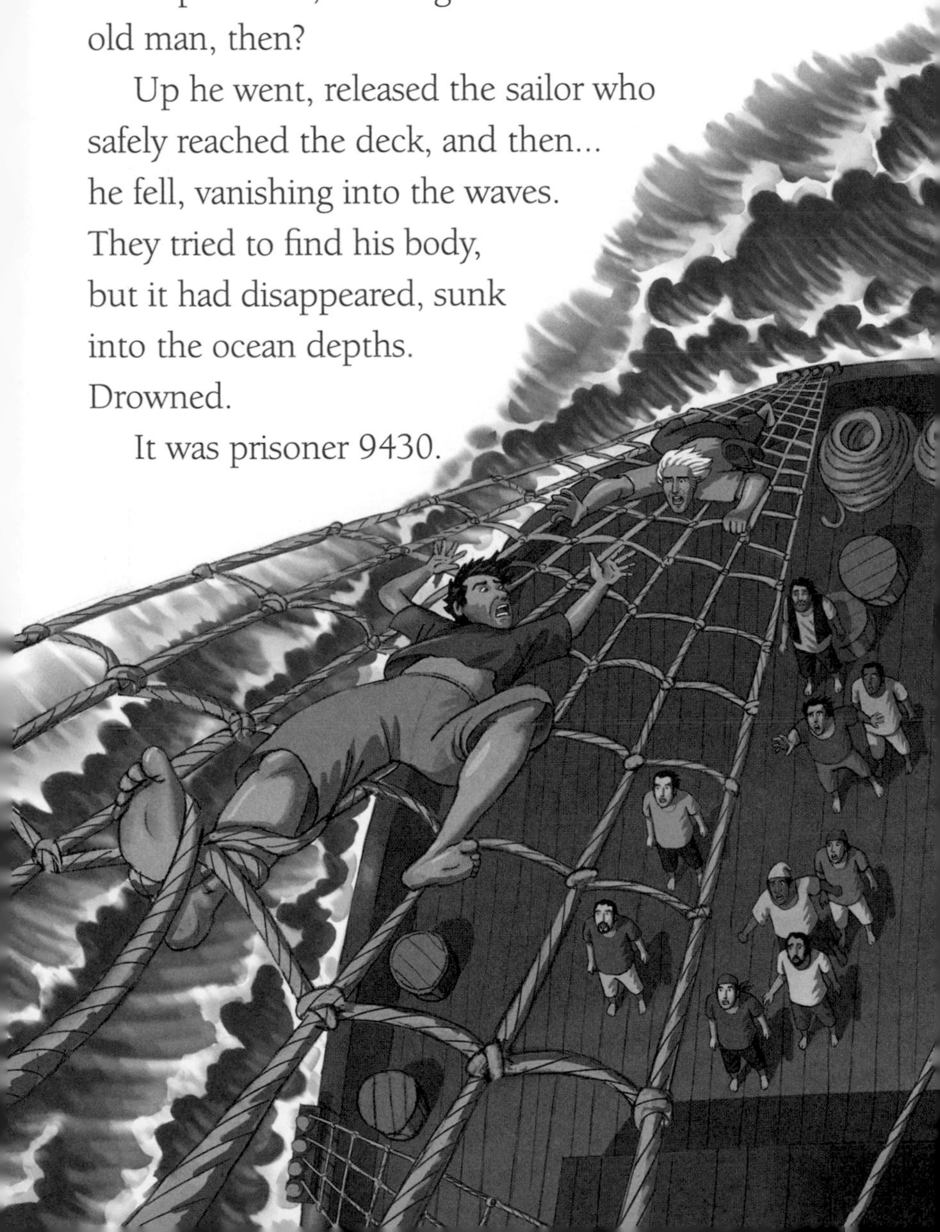

Chapter 4
Saving Cosette

But Valjean was alive. He'd seized his chance, dived into the sea, then swum underwater to hide in an empty boat, moored to a deserted ship, till nightfall. In the still, dark night, he swam along the coast to the nearest town.

From there, he returned to Montreuil to dig up his candlesticks and wallet, buried just where he had left them. He knew he'd be safe. Everyone thought Valjean was dead. Then he bought new clothes for a little girl, and an expensive doll.

At last, he could head for Montfermeil and begin to search for Cosette.

He came across her quite by chance. He had reached the dark woods at the edge of the village at night. There, standing by a stream, was a thin little ragged girl with huge, sad, frightened eyes, struggling to carry a bucket of water. The water slopped and spilled on the ground.

"Child, this is too heavy for you," he said.

"I have to bring it back or they'll beat me."

"Who – your parents? Your parents sent you out in the dark for water?"

"I have none. No, Monsieur and Madame Thénardier will hit me."

"Your name?" urged Valjean, with a gleam of excitement.

"Cosette."

"I will carry your bucket. Lead the way, child."

Cosette was stunned. Someone kind was helping her! No blows, no threats, no beatings... She wasn't used to this. Feeling nervous, she led him to the Thénardiers' inn.

Eponine was playing with a doll.

"Don't come near, don't touch her, Cosette," shrieked Eponine.

"Yes, you're too dirty," Madame Thénardier agreed, giving Cosette a kick. "And what do you want?" she asked Valjean.

"A room for the night. But first, here's a present for this child." Taking out the doll he had bought, he held it up to Cosette.

The doll had long hair, a hat and a velvet coat. Awestruck, Cosette stared rapturously.

"It must have cost a fortune," hissed Madame Thénardier to her husband. "He's crazy to give it to the brat. Is he a millionaire? We'll charge him double for his room."

In the morning, they were certain he was crazy.

"I wish to buy Cosette," Valjean announced.

"But we adore her," Monsieur Thénardier pounced, quick as an adder. "She can't go unless you pay us fifteen hundred francs."

Valjean thrust three bank notes on the table.

Ooh, I'll try for more...I'll make him bribe me, thought Monsieur Thénardier, and whined: "She can't leave without her mother's permission."

Valjean produced the letter Fantine had signed.

There was nothing Thénardier could do except secretly swear to take his revenge somehow, later.

And so Valjean led Cosette away from cruelty and unkindness into a new future. As she clasped Valjean's hand, cuddling her new doll, she felt as she never had before. Safe.

They went to Paris, where Valjean rented an apartment for them.

"It's a bit shabby, I'm afraid," said Valjean.

"It's like heaven," said Cosette. "Shall I sweep the floor?"

"No, child. Play," he told her.

Play? Cosette hardly knew how. She picked up her doll and danced round the room.

As she began to laugh with delight, Valjean felt his soul lift. Valjean had never loved anyone before. He'd never been a father, husband or friend. Long ago, he'd tried to find his own family, but all trace of them had been lost and he'd forgotten them. Prison had taught him to hate. Now, seeing Cosette flowering into happiness, he was learning how to love.

One day, in the backstreets of Paris, Valjean thought he saw Javert.

"Was it really him? Or am I going crazy?" he asked himself. "Maybe because I dread him, I've imagined him. He's not really there."

But that night, he heard footsteps creaking along the corridor. Putting his eye to the keyhole, he saw...Javert! That relentless tracker, come to spy him out, to return Prisoner 9430 to jail.

Valjean shivered. Far worse than prison was the thought of losing Cosette. He simply COULDN'T let her go.

Then the footsteps walked the other way. Javert must have gone to get reinforcements. For the moment, he was safe.

Valjean woke Cosette.

"Time to go," he whispered.

Together they crept silently through the moonlit streets of Paris. It was almost dawn. Glancing behind, Valjean spied Javert following, with two other men. He ran...so did the others. He turned a corner before they did; by his side was a wall; on the other side of the wall was a building.

He climbed. He was good at climbing. Holding Cosette in his arms, using his back, shoulders, knees to secure a toe- or finger-hold, he swarmed up the wall. People, when desperate, move fast.

They slid down to the other side, down a tree branch, into a garden.

"Search!" he heard Javert bellow. "Look in all the streets!"

Safe in the garden, Valjean was still worried, this time about Cosette, trembling in the freezing dawn air. *She must have warmth or she'll die,* he thought.

Then, to his relief, he saw an old gardener, up early, weeding. Before he had time to speak, the old man exclaimed, "Père Madeleine! Did you fall from the skies?"

Valjean was amazed. "Who are you?"

"You don't know? You saved my life, when that cart nearly crushed me, and you got me this job here in the convent. I'm Fauchelevent."

Valjean thought rapidly. "Now you can save MY life. Will you hide me here? And the child?"

"Come to my cottage," said Fauchelevent. "No one will know. No one can enter the convent without permission."

He took them to his fireside, where Cosette settled down to sleep, rosy in the warmth.

Valjean and Cosette spent the next five years there. In the silent peace of the quiet garden and the cloisters, surrounded by caring nuns, and seeing Cosette so happy, Valjean felt he'd been given another chance. His heart melted in gratitude, and his love for Cosette grew.

Chapter 5
Cosette in Love

Fauchelevent died, and Valjean and Cosette left the sanctuary of the convent.

After all these years, Valjean thought, *we will surely be safe from Javert.*

They rented an apartment near a park where they walked every day. This park was also the chosen spot of a young man, named Marius.

He soon noticed the fatherly old man and his lovely laughing daughter. Marius spoke to Cosette every afternoon, and swiftly fell in love with her.

Marius lived in a shabby tenement building – by coincidence, the same one that Monsieur and Madame Thénardier had moved to from Montfermeil, with their daughter, Eponine.

They had stopped being innkeepers, but they were still liars. Marius knew how they got their money. They wrote begging letters under a false name.

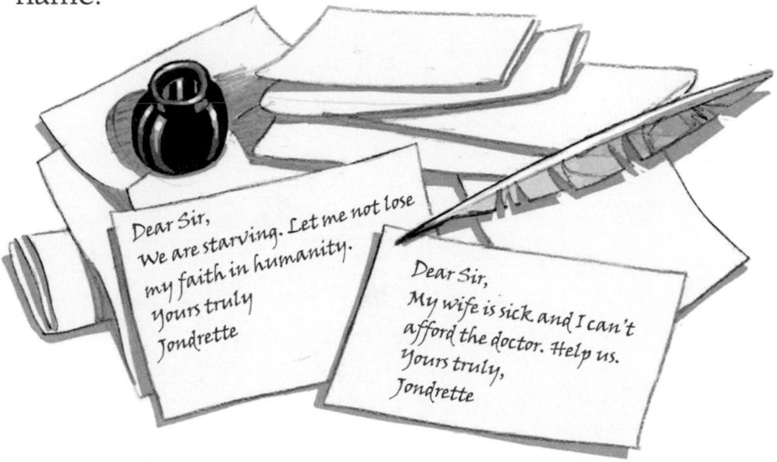

Eponine was in love with Marius, but she knew he thought only of Cosette. Eponine had seen them together, though she didn't tell a soul. She hated Cosette. *That brat who ate our scraps. Now she's dressed in silks and I'm the one in rags,* she thought. *And the man I love won't look at me because of her.*

Marius was friends with a group of men known as the ABC, a rebel gang who wanted to get rid of the monarchy and make France a Republic once more.

"Why do they want to fight?" asked Eponine.

"The rich are too rich and the poor too poor. Revolution is the only answer," replied Marius, his eyes alight with fire as he seized a rifle. "We have to banish famine and disease. This is the only way... Long live freedom and equality!"

But Eponine only wished he'd kiss her.

One morning, Marius saw Cosette and Valjean handing a fistful of clinking coins to Thénardier. Marius realized the old crook must have sent Valjean one of his begging letters.

“Hey,” hissed Madame Thénardier into her husband’s ear. “I’m sure that’s Cosette – and the man who took her. They haven’t recognized us!”

“I’ll get him to come back tomorrow,” Thénardier whispered back. “Then I’ll kill him. I promised myself I’d take my revenge one day.”

Marius heard every word and raced to the police, to tell them of the murder plot. The chief policeman was none other than Javert.

“I’ll catch the old villain,” muttered Javert. “AT LAST...!” and Marius, of course, didn’t know that Javert was referring to Valjean.

The next day, when Valjean and Cosette turned up at Thénardier's apartment, Javert was there, waiting for them, hiding behind the wooden window shutters.

"Ah!" crowed Thénardier. "My noble philanthropist! My wealthy buyer of dolls! Don't you recognize me? The innkeeper of Montfermeil. You got the better of me once. But not now!"

Javert jumped out and seized Valjean, but Valjean had not lost his skills. Twisting like an eel, he slipped out of his grasp and leaped from a window.

Cosette fled too. When they no longer returned to the park each day, Marius was distraught.

"Help me find her," he implored Eponine.

Weeks passed. Paris was in meltdown, with Marius's friends talking about building barricades in the city and leading a rebellion. They met every night to plan, but Marius was too in love to care.

Finally, Eponine came to Marius. "I don't know the address but I've found out where they're living."

Marius began meeting Cosette in secret and she fell in love with him. He didn't know Eponine was following in disguise, watching them jealously. Then, one night, Marius went to meet Cosette, and found the house deserted. Thinking she no longer loved him, he headed to his friends in despair and joined the rebellion. Silently, Eponine followed.

It was June 5th, 1832, and the rebels had called for action. They were manning a ramshackle barricade, facing the army. Just then, a shot rang out, fatally wounding Eponine.

As she lay dying, Marius held her in his arms.

"Don't leave me," she gasped, her face twisted with pain. "I have a confession. I met Cosette and she gave me a letter for you but I kept it. Take it."

She grasped Marius's hand and pulled it to her pocket.

Bewildered, he drew out the letter. Then Eponine cried out and he held her close. Her last moments were full of joy, believing that she was loved by him at last.

Gently, Marius laid Eponine down on the ground and read the letter.

My dearest! We leave for England in a week. Until then we are at 7, Rue de L'Homme Armé.

Marius's heart gave a leap. *She still loves me,* he thought. *I must tell her that I have given my life to the rebellion now, but she will always have my heart.*

He quickly scribbled a note and gave it to a boy who was near the barricade.

"Please take this and deliver it as soon as you can," he begged. He had done all he could. The rest was up to fate.

Chapter 6
The Greatness of Valjean

Fate was on his side, for Valjean saw the boy arrive and read the note. He raced through the streets, thinking: *Marius truly loves Cosette and she loves him. I must see that he comes to no harm...*

Arriving at the barricade, Valjean was amazed to see Javert, who had been captured by the rebels as a spy.

"Here," one of them shouted to Valjean, thinking he was a rebel too. "Take this man and kill him for us."

Valjean took Javert down an alleyway and untied the ropes binding the policeman's arms. "You're free. Go, Javert."

Javert couldn't believe his ears. He owed his life to a criminal. A man he had hunted. And this man had shown kindness and mercy. Everything was topsy turvy. It made him shudder. Where was order? Justice? Regulations?

Javert couldn't cope. He felt there was no place for him in a world where evil was repaid by good. He had to admire Valjean. He felt himself a lesser man. His belief in himself, his life and the way he had lived it...all lay in ruins.

He walked to the river, where it flows in a dangerous rapid. He looked down and leaned forward...

There was a splash. And that was all.

Valjean had returned to the barricade to check on Marius. The worst had happened. The rebels were losing badly and were dead or dying. Marius, too, had been hurt and lay unmoving. Valjean leaped on him like a tiger protecting a cub and carried him to safety.

Shots were being fired in all directions, but it was clear to Valjean that it would all soon be over. The brief rebellion had come to nothing.

I must get Marius to safety, he thought.

But where? Death lurked round every corner.

A possibility emerged: an iron grille set in the pavement. Using all his strength, Valjean pulled up the grille. Beneath it was a flue-like chimney, going down and down...

Heaving Marius over his shoulder, Valjean descended, until he found himself in a long, underground passage. He was in the sewers of Paris.

A sewer is a muck heap. It's like the darkest side of life, where rats roam, trinkets are lost and secrets are thrown away.

Valjean carried Marius, not knowing if he was alive or dead. He didn't know where he was going, only onwards, away from the heart of Paris, sinking deeper into the stinking filth.

Slowly it crept up his body, covering his ankles, his knees, his shoulders, his neck...

Terrible to die like this.

Valjean found himself thinking not of himself or Marius, but of Cosette.

At last, he found he was by another grille. But this time, he couldn't open it. It was locked.

"Don't worry," said a voice. "I've got a key."

It was Thénardier, searching in the sewer for whatever he could find, another rat among many. "I see you've killed a man," grinned Thénardier. He didn't recognize Valjean, but he felt friendly to one he assumed was just like himself. "Give me what he has in his pockets and I'll open the grille."

Valjean nodded, realizing Thénardier supposed him to be a murderer.

"You can throw the body in the river. He'll never be discovered," said Thénardier, emptying Marius's pockets and unlocking the grille. "Only a few coins. You didn't murder for much!"

Valjean staggered through the grille. He was free! He laid Marius down on the ground. Marius was alive – and just breathing. Valjean brought him back to his own house and to Cosette.

In time, Marius recovered. He knew he'd been rescued from the sewer, but not who his rescuer was. Valjean never told him.

Marius and Cosette married, and Valjean gave them all his money. But things didn't work out happily ever after. Cosette and Marius loved each other – of that there was no doubt. But Marius wouldn't let Cosette visit Valjean, because Valjean had told him about the time he'd spent in prison.

"He's a common criminal," Marius told Cosette. "A disgrace. Shameful."

Cosette was desperately unhappy. She looked on Valjean as her father. Meanwhile, Valjean grew old, weak and lonely.

Things might have stayed that way, but Thénardier decided to get money out of Marius.

"I know a secret about Valjean," he declared. "There's no point in me going to him. You've got all his money. But you can give some of it to me, to keep quiet about your wife's father. He might have spared Javert, and I heard he was Père Madeleine, so he did some good, but the man is a murderer. Ha! I saw him in the sewer, carrying a dead body."

"Then HE saved my life? I owe my life to him!" cried Marius. "Go away, Thénardier. I cannot bear to look at you."

He called out to Cosette, urging her to come with him to see her father at once.

Marius reproached himself bitterly. Everything he had believed about Valjean was wrong. His father-in-law was a hero.

Chapter 7
Goodbye

At Valjean's house, Cosette fell into his arms and hugged him. "Father!"

"Come and live with us," said Marius.

"Yes, come home and eat strawberries with us in the garden, and we'll see each other every day..." laughed Cosette, taking his hands in hers. "But why are you so cold, Father?"

"I have not long to live," murmured Valjean. "Come close. I love you both dearly. How sweet it is to die surrounded by such love."

"No, Father. I can't lose you!" cried Cosette.

"Do not weep. I won't be far away. I shall be watching over you. Do you remember the doll I bought you, Cosette? I remember your child's eyes, your laughter..."

"I remember everything," wept Cosette. "Father...Father... "

"You were an enchanting child," said Valjean. "And now the time has come to tell you your mother's name. Fantine. She loved you, and she suffered. She was as rich in sorrow as you are in happiness. Remember her name; speak of her with respect. And love each other always. Nothing matters in this world except love."

Cosette and Marius knelt down, one each side of him. He did not move again, but lay with his head turned to the sky. The sun, shining in, reflected off two silver candlesticks to fall on his face, peaceful at last.

Background to the story

Les Misérables opens in 1815, when famine, disease and poverty ravaged France. The French Revolution, which began in 1789, had seen the king, Louis XVI, and his wife, Marie Antoinette, beheaded. Thousands of aristocrats were sent to the guillotine too. This period was called the Reign of Terror.

A young general, Napoleon, rose through the ranks, conquering countries for France and becoming its Emperor. After Napoleon's defeat at Waterloo, the royal family was reinstated, but unrest and unhappiness continued and, with them, the wish for further revolution.

The events in *Les Misérables* are set during the reigns of the new kings, Louis XVIII, Charles X and Louis-Philippe. The novel follows the history of France up to the 'June rebellion', which lasted for just two days on the 5th and 6th June in 1832. This is the fight in which Marius's friends, the fictional ABC gang, take part.

Usborne Quicklinks

For links to websites where you can find out more about *Les Misérables,* its author, Victor Hugo, and life in France at the time, go to the Usborne Quicklinks website at **www.usborne.com/quicklinks** and enter the keywords *Les Miserables*.

Please follow the internet safety guidelines at the Usborne Quicklinks website. We recommend that children are supervised while on the internet.

Victor Hugo 1802-1885

Victor Hugo was born in eastern France, two years before Napoleon declared himself Emperor. Victor's father fought for Napoleon so he spent his early childhood journeying around Europe.

Victor wrote poetry and plays as well as novels, but he is especially known for two of his stories – *The Hunchback of Notre Dame,* and *Les Misérables*, which has been made into numerous films and a world-famous musical.

With thanks to Lottie Sims
Digital manipulation: John Russell & Nick Wakeford
Series designer: Russell Punter

First published in 2018 by Usborne Publishing Ltd., Usborne House, 83-85 Saffron Hill, London EC1N 8RT, England. www.usborne.com